SPECIAL THANKS FOR USE OF PHOTO
BY
STEVE'S CREATIONS At Pixabay.com

Shredded Bodies

Christopher Ridge

Published by Christopher Ridge, 2023.

This is a work of fiction. Similarities to real people, places, or events are entirely coincidental.

SHREDDED BODIES

First edition. July 15, 2023.

Copyright © 2023 Christopher Ridge.

ISBN: 979-8215992104

Written by Christopher Ridge.

Table of Contents

SHREDDED BODIES

Dick turned the wheel of the white Hyundai Sonata straight into on coming traffic going head on with a tractor trailer.

Dick isn't his real name. Should be but it isn't.

Jane isn't really Jane either but we're calling her that to protect her identity for marrying such a dumbass.

Jane was sleeping because she trusted her husband, Dick. She trusted him like a dog turning over for its owner for a belly rub. She didn't know that Dick had secrets of his own. Little did she know what Dick was about to do at the time.

They were on their way to celebrate their anniversary of fourteen years. Going to spend the weekend at a fancy hotel with a nice pool and have sex in a Jacuzzi in Ohio. They were having marriage problems and Dick thought it would be a good way to get things in order.

Jane had a special kind of trust so strong a foundation it was the kind marriages were supposed to be built of before society said it was okay to part ways if you're not happy.

She was too good for Dick.

Way too good.

Everybody tried to tell her he was bad news. She wouldn't listen. She thought she knew Dick. She thought she knew.

Well, she didn't know this.

Dick had slept with twenty other women. Including her sister and her best friend. Three of them he got pregnant, but he got them all aborted with all the big big money he made as a heart surgeon.

Like he wanted Jane to do but Jane was having this baby. She can't believe he has it in him to do something like that.

He tries to play it off like we shouldn't make others suffer by bringing them into this hard cruel world and thinks they will be better off.

Dick done this so many times it was easy-pessy.

That's because she really didn't know Dick was really a dick.

She also didn't know he had another waiting at the hotel they were staying at. This was going to be his weekend. Party it up and live like a rock star as he liked to say.

He and Jane were staying on the fourth floor while the other waited on the second floor that way it would decrease their chances of running into each other.

The funny thing about it was, Jane knew this woman. She had lunch with her several times.

Dick would be happy if he wasn't such a well, D.I.C.K.

The horn echoed through the midnight and all Dick saw was the blinding bright headlights shining upon him as if he was on a stage performing.

This was showtime.

The moment of truth.

The moment Dick finally set things straight and this was his way of fixing the problem.

Except for that split second, he thought, oh shit. I just screwed this up. He'd done crossed over to the other side. Crossed the line an there was no turning back.

Everything moved in slow motion as if he were watching this all unfold before his eyes and there was nothing he could do about it to change it.

He turned the wheel to the right but he knew there nothing he was going to be able to do to change it.

Jane wakes, eyes wide, mouth wide but at that point could only scream. Her fingers claw into the side of the seat, digging deeper and deeper into the cushion as if she were holding on to the edge of a cliff by the tips of her fingers.

Her legs straight out as she presses the floor as if she were going to stop the car.

Dick holds the wheel tight. White knuckles. Arms straight out. He knows it too late. Too late to do anything about it.

In the short second all this took he thinks about how sorry is for doing this. If God somehow managed to forgive him in case he happens to get lucky and survive this, he promises to himself he will come clean and tell Jane everything. She deserves at least that.

The lights get closer.

Closer.

The trucker's horn blares.

Dick's heart beats quick like it's going to come through his chest. He feels something in his throat trying to get out.

He glances over at Jane. She screams her head off. Really screams her head off.

They both hear the sound of crunching metal and plastic. Damn cars these days crumble like a coffee cake.

They smell smoke. See smoke. His arms burn.

Is the car on fire?

Should we get out of here?

Not yet.

A large tree branch come through the windshield and impales the baby inside Jane belly.

The baby feels something stabbing at it but can't do anything about it.

The car rolls.

Jane flies through the windshield like a bullet.

Her head rolls around on the seat. Still screaming. He heard the brain is still active for a short while once decapitated.

Jane's head screaming as if she is very much aware of what is going on.

The car rolls. He lost track after the third time.

Crunching. Smashing.

The other half of June's torso is sticking out of the front windshield. Her feet dangling over the dashboard. Large streams of blood travel down her leg and drip from the tips of her bloody toes and is splattering everywhere and all over Dick's face.

He hears a loud explosion as large shards of glass splattering all over inside as if a bomb went off.

He feels scratching all over his face and his arms.

His eyes hurt. Hurt like hell. He feels something cool around them.

He can't see.

The car is still rolling. When is this all going to stop? At this point he knows he's going to die. This is going to be it. Soon God will pull the curtain shut.

When?

As soon as he gets his reward, he hears a voice say. The voice is deep, dark and sounded like a demon as if it were the Grim

Reaper himself coming to collect. You get what you get and don't throw a fit.

He feels something smack into his head. He can't see it but its June's head still banging around.

Tree branches burst through the windshield. Dick feels something impale his chest.

At first it hurt. Then it stopped. Only a burning sensation as he coughs and spits and the blood in his throat causing him to gurgle.

He wonders why does all this have to happen?

It was his reward to die this way. God's cruel joke on mankind.

He just wants out, out of all this mess.

Well, he gets out. Dick is thrown twenty feet. Mother karma tossing him around like the ragdoll he is.

He faintly hears a soft crack as his head smashed into a tree.

The car finally comes to a rest at the bottom of a hill.

Wheels still turning and squeaking. Ironically the music is still blaring on the radio.

The bodies of Dick and Jane are scattered.

Jane is lying in two different places.

Her head is stuck in the trees. Her torso lies on the ground. She is on her back. Her belly sliced open exposing the baby. His feet still kicking. It will stop soon. He gives a few yelps looking for his mama but mama cannot hear him.

It will stop soon.

Dick is lying on the ground. His right arm is severed at the elbow and is hanging on a tree branch by its fingertips.

The right side of his face is smashed in.

They are not going to be easy to find at the bottom of the hill down in the ditch. Maybe some hunters will accidentally stumble upon them.

James life ripped away in a matter of seconds. All her hopes and dreams of being a good mother and wife are gone. This was all she ever wanted and needed.

She may be in heaven with her daughter in arms saying. Thanks Dick.

THE KILL ROOM

Webster woke looking at dark brown 4x4 wood beams. He wanted to move. Desperately. His back ached as bad as that time he was sick in bed for three days. He bit down on some rubber ball object shoved in his mouth like he were a roasting pig.

Ohhhh, great. This is just great. People who wake up with things strapped to their mouth never has a good ending

He felt something cold on his back. A single light bulb dangling from a cord flickered.

His nose itched.

He smelled mildew and piss.

Where am I?

He knew this wasn't good. No way could it be good.

His head pulsed and ached like an over inflated basketball.

I can't move.

My arms. What's going on with my arms? And my feet.

Tried moving his legs but his legs wouldn't move.

He can't see.

I've got to get up. Move around. Arms and legs felt crampy like he had been at his desk for hours at work in the phone company.

He also noticed he was naked. Oh, God. This is so not good. He tried thinking back about how he got here. Obviously, he was here because somebody wanted to do him harm.

From the looks of it he was in some sort of madman's torture chamber. But he didn't know why.

Why am I here?

Obviously, you pissed somebody off, said the voice inside his head.

He thought back to all the possibilities of who his capture could possibly be. Not a clue.

Not one.

Judging by this situation he was in this was going to be bad. Very bad.

How long have I been here? Surely, Janet would report I'm missing when I don't come home for dinner. I'm always home at five. No later than six. She'll call for help and somebody will come and get me out of this.

The itch above his forehead kept picking at him like a bug was digging deep into his flesh.

Is it too late to pray?

I've never been a praying man but maybe God will hear me and get me out of this.

Ohh, God. I ask you. Please save my soul now. Please get me out of this.

This was useless. God ain't coming to help you out of this when you've never went to church since you were twelve. Face it, pal. You're screwed.

This was not funny. This voice in his head had a sick sense of humor.

Something squeaked to his right.

What is that?

He turned his head slightly to the right. Straining his eyes looking down as far as they could possibly go.

SQUEAK SQUEAK SQUEAK

A rat.

He could hear it pitter pattering up the bench leg.

Oh, God. It's coming up here.

Get away. Get away, he screamed. Shoo shooo. He felt its nasty greasy hair rubbing next to his body.

It stopped. Squeaked.

What's it doing now?

I hate rats. It reminded him of the time his grandfather caught one in the basement of the old house and how he held it by its tail. The thing was big as a cat. A real New York rat he called it.

Owwww. Something pinched me.

What's it doing?

Owwww. Did it again. This time it really hurt.

Its biting me. Stop it. Just stop it. Like it was really going to listen.

He wiggled and squirmed trying to get the rat away from him.

Think back. Where was I? Oh jeez.

Can't remember.

C'mon. Surely you remember where you were last night or yesterday.

This is so weird.

It was a usual day. Got showered, Janet was still sleeping.

Ok. Nothing unusual there.

It's hot here. Like a furnace.

Janet and I been having some differences lately.

Nothing unusual there. All married couples have a spat or two from time to time. She wouldn't want to though. This would be taking things too far.

Okay.

Did I leave the office? Don't remember.

Oh, God. If you're up there, please help me remember.

Did I piss somebody off?

Probably. I'm all the time pissing someone off. Part of the job as a financial advisor. There's been a few unhappy clients.

His father tried telling him that making a living g off other hardworking people's back was no way to make a living. His father never liked his job and believed it to be dishonest and immoral.

The lock clicked.

The blackened brass doorknob jiggled.

The door squeaked softly on its rusty hinges as it was pushed open by someone he couldn't see.

Footsteps clicked on the floor and he heard splashing water

A pretty woman with long red hair came into view.

She smiled as if this were a special treat. A gift.

She had big tits. They jiggled when she walked. If I had met her in a bar, I'd for sure make a move on her. For some reason I don't think I'm her type.

A man in a black suit comes in, hands her a white plastic apron. "Thank you for visiting us at the Kill Room, Mrs. Thompson."

Ok. So, her name is Mrs. Thompson. Not good he said her name in front of him.

Thinking back he didn't know anybody named Thompson. Never even saw this woman before.

Maybe she knows me.

The kill room? What is this?

"Thank you so much. I've been looking forward to this. Had the urge to kill this bastard from the first moment I saw him at the intersection honking his horn behind me because I didn't move at the green light fast enough."

The man chuckles and claps his hands. "And there he is. All nice and fresh for you. We're glad we can be of service. We here at the Kill Room want to make sure our customers get the full experience of, well, killing of course. It's an experience like no other."

She glanced around at the tray of tools on the cart as she tied the apron around her back and looked at Webster. "He is just perfect. Absolutely perfect."

"Nice to hear. We have the best of the best scouts out around the area constantly on the lookout for our orders as they come in."

"And so fast "

The man smiled. He had all gold teeth. "We aim to please here at the Kill room. And for your $250,000, we've added an even more special selection of tools of your choice."

What? She paid 250,000 to kill me in this room? Why? Surely, there must be some sort of mistake here. Mistaken me for someone else.

Webster squirms and wiggles, and groans. His heart racing in his chest. He tries to tell them to stop. He wants a chance to explain before she continues with this nonsense but the only thing coming out of his mouth was slurred speech and grunts because of the ball gag

She looked at her server. "I love it when they squirm and wiggle like that."

"Ahhh, yes. We make sure our products are nice and fresh for our customers. Well, I'll leave you to it. Just push the red button on the wall if you need me."

"Thank you so much."

"Of course. It's my pleasure."

Webster hated that saying. Seems like everyone is saying that these days.

There's something seriously wrong with this. They act like this is normal. Nothing normal about this and clearly this wasn't this woman's first time.

This gag has to come out. He had questions. Lots of questions.

"My. You do look delicious lying here all naked and at the ready. I'll make sure this is going to be slow and painful because I like my men slow and in pain "

His speech came out slurred but what he was saying was , "You're a sick bitch."

"What was that sweetie? Sounded like you called me a something bitch? Sick perhaps? Psycho? Naa. Nothing psycho bout this, sweetie. This is life's greatest stress reliefs. Killing is an exhilarating experience. At least for those of us who have the money to do it that is." She held up a small five pound sledge. "No worries. We're going to start off light."

She brought the hammer down on his left hand. Webster felt an instant shot of pain radiating up his arm and tingled around the back of his neck

She slammed it again and again. The bones in his hand shattering as she whacked and whacked and whacked.

He screamed and screamed. His body twisting any which way he could against the restraints in attempt to get away.

"Ooooo Weeeeeee. This feels so awesome." She gave his hand two more whacks and went to work on the other. "Worth every bit of it "

His back arched as she whacked and whacked. He saw her smiling as his blood splattered on her face. "Mmmmm...Mmmmmm...." Tears running down the side of his face.

"Mmmmm...Mmmmmm. Good is right, Sweetie." She lifted his hand that now looked as flat as she could possibly make it. "Oh, look. You have a boo boo. Don't you worry, Sweetie. Mommy will fix it."

She grabbed an electric tree limb saw. Bone and gristle and flesh splattered on her face and apron as she sliced off his hand.

Then she cut off the other

Mushroom clouds of blood erupting from the stumps.

A knock at the door just as his hand fell to the floor

It was the server. "Just checking on you to see if you need anything." His gaze shifted to Webster and smiled at all the blood. "Looks like things are going well "

"Very well, "she said.

"Good then. Let me know if you need anything."

"I sure will. Thank you so much."

"It's my pleasure "

These people are insane. Psychopaths. I've been captured my maniacs in some sort of rich man's secret club.

"Just hang in there, Sweetie. We're almost done." She removed a very hot iron and placed it on the bleeding stumps.

His skin sizzled. Cracked and popped. "That should do for now. At least it slowed the bleeding down."

She studied the other tools on the tray. "Let's see. What should we play with next?"

Webster moaned. Groaned. Wishing by now she would just kill him and get this madness over with.

"Let's see. How bout this?" She picked up a small ball peen hammer. She slapped it in her hand. "Yes. I believe this will suffice "First we have to remove this ball and strap. This has been in you for a while you poor thing. "

Yes, he thought. Take it off. About time. I've got some questions.

His eyes widened with excitement as she leaned over and unbuckled the strap. Her tits touching his face and he didn't know much about perfumes but she sure smelled great for a woman who was about to kill him.

What can I do? Have to do something. Take my chances. Obviously, screaming ain't going to help. That will draw too much attention.

"Let's get this out of your mouth so you can breathe, Sweetie."

This was his chance to try something. Anything. His heart quickened with excitement.

Just as she grabbed the gag he jerked his head lashing out at her fingers.

He bit with the force of a pit bull. It was a now or never type situation. He bit as hard as he could, growling and shaking his head as his teeth tore into her flesh and he felt the crackly of her fingers. The taste of blood on his tongue.

She screamed and punched him in the face until he let go. "You're a feisty fella, aren't ya. That's good. I like'm nice and feisty.

She climbed on top of him. Grabbed the small pick from the tray and inserted the point of the pick in the center of his left eye.

Deeper and deeper.

Blood oozed out from between the socket and the pick making a sucking sound as she drove it deeper and deeper until she reached the center of his brain.

His legs twitching. Arms shaking.

Next, she went to work on the other eye.

Now, he wasn't going to be able to see what she was going to do to him. Can only feel.

He heard the revving of what sounded like a battery powered saws-all. He'd recognized that sound because his grandfather always used one when working around cars.

He felt the teeth tearing into his shoulder and felt the blade as it cut deep and deeper into his shoulder. Then she went to work on his other arm but by then he was gone and all the cutting wasn't fun anymore.

A knock at the door. The server glanced around. "I see all went well with your service."

"Very well. Couldn't be better."

He glanced at her fingers. "Looks like things had gotten a little rough."

"It did. But I like'm rough. Rough and squealing."

He grinned and handed her a towel. "Let's get you to the nurse's station and get you all fixed up ."

"Thank you so much."

"I'm happy to be of service. Please stop by and see us again "

"I most certaintly will. You can count on it "

"Great. Also, would you mind filling out the brief survey in your email? You will also get twenty-five percent off on your next service. We always enjoy hearing from our satisfied customers."

"Love to. Thank so much."

"It's my pleasure."

GRANPA'S GOT A CHAINSAW

"**O**h, wow. What's he doing with it?"

"Nothing. Just cutting down some old tree around his yard."

"Ohhh. That's cool. His yard needing cleaned up anyway."

"Does he need any help?"

"No. He said he was fine and don't need help."

"Ohhh. Ok."

"Hey, Granpa has a chainsaw."

"Ohhh, no. That's not good."

'No."

"What's he doing with it?"

"He chopped up the neighbor that has been picking on him for all these years. You know the one that has been giving him a hard time about his trees branches hanging over on his side of the fence."

"Ohh. Well, that guy probably deserved it. Everybody hated him."

"Fella met his match with grandpa."

"You ain't kidding."

"Did somebody call the cops?"

"I don't think anybody saw him doing it. I'm going to help him bury the body."

"Cool."

"Did you know grandpa has a chainsaw?"

"What's going on now?"

"Nothing. He's oiling it and sharpening the blade getting it ready for the next job."

"I see. I surprised nobody took it away from him yet."

"Grandpa is attached to that chainsaw."

"Hey, grandpa has a chainsaw."

"What's he doing now?"

"He cut a burglar's head off last night while he was trying to break into his house."

"Good for him. Been a lot of break-ins in that neighborhood lately."

"Made quite a mess though. There's blood everywhere."

"Didn't get on grandma's favorite sofa did it? You know that was her favorite sofa."

"No. Thank Goodness. Grandpa did it in the kitchen on the linoleum floor."

"That's good. Glad everything worked out."

"I hate to ask this but what did he do with the rest of the body?"

"You really want to know?"

"I... I... Think so."

"He cut up the body into tiny pieces and shoved them down the garbage disposal."

"Wow. I bet that was messy."

"You don't know the half of it."

"I'm helping him clean up the mess now."

"Grandpa has a chainsaw."

"Oh no. He still has that thing?"

"Of course."

"What's he doing with it?"

"Not much today. Just doing some preventive maintenance, oiling, cleaning and wiping it down. He said his name is, Bubba. Then he and Bubba took a nap."

"That's a relief. At least he's getting his rest."

"Granpa has a chainsaw."

"Ok. You've got to be kidding me."

"Nope. Afraid not."

"What's he doing with it?"

"He cut up a dog that kept pooping in his yard."

"Grandpa sure hate dogs. Which one was it?"

"Maggie's Border Collie down the street? Yeah, that one."

"That cute little dog?'

"You know how grandpa hates dogs."

"Ohhh, you ain't kidding."

"Did the old lady get mad?"

"She doesn't know yet."

"That's so sad "

"That's grandpa for ya "

"Grandpas got a chainsaw."

"Oh no. What's he doing with it?

"He's trimming the trees of that lady's house who's dog he cut up "

"So he does have a heart "

"Seems that way "

"Does she know it was him?"

"I don't think so."

"Probably better that way."

"Grandpas got a chainsaw."

"Oh my. What's he doing with it?

"He cut off some kids head who wasn't from this neighborhood and thought he was a burglar.*

"Was he?*

"No. His family just moved in two days ago "

"Wow. So sad for that family."

"That's grandpa for ya "

"Grandpa's got a chainsaw."

"Oh no.What's he doing with it?"

"He's oiling the chain and making her look all nice and shiny telling her what a good girl she is."

"He said he's putting her to bed so she can get some rest. Said she has a big day tomorrow."

"That sure sounds scary "

"Your telling me "

"What do you think he's gonna do?"

"I have no idea."

"To be honest, I don't think I want to know."

"Ne either "

"Grandpas got a chainsaw."

"I thought you said it was sleeping "

"Grandpa woke her up "

"Oh great. What's he doing with it"

"You don't want to know. Seriously. You don't "

"Probably better off not knowing anyway "

"Yep. You are. I was up all night burying the bodies. I'm exhausted."

"For such an old man he sure is high maintenance."

"Grandpas got a chainsaw."

"What's that ole coot doing with it now!"

"He's smashing it into a million pieces."

"I've got to say I didn't see that coming."

"Yeah, he said he was tired of it talking to him like that."

"Talking to him like what?"

" I don't know. Bossy I guess. Like it was his wife or something."

"Cant blame him for that "

"I helped him bury it last night. He had a priest pray and everything. He wanted to make sure he'd do t right "

"Good riddance"

"Finally it's over "

"Amen to that."

"Grandpa's got a chainsaw "

"Seriously? Another one!"

"Yeo "

"Whats he doing with it?"

"Said he found it on his front porch this morning."

THE SQUATTER

"**I** don't believe it. I just don't believe it. Looks like somebody is using the house," Herbert said. He had the drape pulled back on the side window just enough to keep an eye on him.

"Is that right?" His wife, June said. "About time somebody moves into that house. Be nice to have some good neighbors. I hope they're good people. Do they look like good people?"

"Looks like he's squatting."

"Seriously?"

"That's what it looks like to me."

Herbert was keeping an eye on him because he had seen him walking around here for two days. Somebody that is not from the neighborhood tends to stand out. He tried talking to him a few times but all he does is turn his head as if he did not want to be bothered.

Herbert was more curious so he had been keeping an eye on things for the last couple of days.

There was no car, that he knew of. He saw a young woman around a few times but that could have been his wife.

He was kind of tall but not quite six feet. From the color of his skin, he looked like he was from India.

But India people tend to have big families and live with uncles and aunts and their kids and all their kids all in once house. Plus, work at gas stations.

It ticked Herbert off that so many people from India and Pakistan were given all this money to put up a gas station on practically every corner. To make things worse they don't even pay taxes.

It makes no sense.

The more Herbert thought about it the more infuriated he became.

"Now, don't you go getting yourself all worked up over that man. You know the doctor told you to watch your blood pressure."

Herbert stomped into the kitchen, opened the fridge, closed it, felt his stomach rumble but didn't get anything. "It's kind of hard to do when you have people like that squatting."

"I'll make a call to the rental company tomorrow."

"Nobody knows this guy and we don't know if he really belongs there. Wait. You think he may have something to do with all the break ins lately?"

"I don't know, honey. I doubt it."

"Well, I don't."

The man was now sitting in a lawn chair in front of the garage and scrolling on his phone.

Yesterday when Herbert got home from work he was cleaning the garage floor.

This was all weird.

Last week a nice young couple were looking at the house and asked Herbert if anybody had been scammed on this house. The young couple saw the house on Facebook and called the number and the guy wanted them to Vemo him a deposit.

So, something weird was going on.

The man just sat there as if he was living there.

Herbert grabbed a beer from the fridge and took a large gulp. "That's what they do you know. Those squatters. They take over vacant houses. The next thing you know prostitutes are running around and drug dealers.

It was irritating that so many houses in the development were going up for sale and being bought by rental companies. When Herbert and June first bought the house this was a nice neighborhood, hardly any trouble and they were told that there were not going to be any rentals. Most of the time, not always but most of the time there is a huge difference between people who rent and people that own.

That evening, after dinner, Herbert took the trash out. This time there was a tan car int the driveway. He was wiping it down.

Herbert looked at him hoping to make some sort of eye contact in hopes of starting a conversation so he could find out a little more about him. Oh, who was he kidding, he wanted to know a lot more.

June thought that maybe it was legit. Maybe he was the new neighbor moving in but Herbert wasn't having any of it.

He wanted neighbors but he wanted good neighbors and he didn't want to live next door to a bunch of unfriendly foreigners.

Just the other day he saw him walking down Troy Ave. down by the farms. He was walking in sandals and carrying two small plastic bags, one in each hand. Herbert wondered what he was doing walking around out there considering there was nothing but cornfields.

He could've cut across the fields over on Arlington but then he would've had to go through the Stratford apartments and you did not want to walk through the drug ridden, crack dealing

Stratford's. Herbert didn't even like the idea of them being so close.

He came back inside. "I think we should think about moving."

June stopped drying the dish and froze. "You want to do what?"

"I'm thinking about moving. This neighborhood is going down hill and now they're putting up another gas station on the corner of Arlington and Troy. We already have four, two on each corner all within a mile of each other. And you know what that means? And don't even get me started on the liquor store and pawn shop that went in three years ago."

"What's that?" She hated to ask.

"More robberies. This neighborhood is going to hell in a handbasket."

"All this started over the guy we think may be a squatter."

"That's right. That's how this all starts. Next thing you know we've turned into the ghetto. I could've sworn I heard gunshots last night."

"That could've been the farmer shooting coyotes. I saw on the new that there's and overabundance of them."

"Naaaa. I don't think that's what it was." He stomped around the living room waving his arms frantically as if the world was coming to an end. "I think somebody got shot. That's what I think."

"Honey, I don't think so. We would've heard something on the news."

"They don't put everything on the news honey. Sometimes they leave out all the good stuff."

Herbert pulled the curtain back.

"Is he still there?" June asked.

"No. He's gone. Must've went inside."

What's the neighbor doing now?

Herbert kept a close watch on the house for the next three days. All the while he saw the neighbor come and go.

Herbert wanted so desperately to talk to him but the guy would not give him the time of day which made Herbert feel that something even more shady was going on.

Who was this guy?

Where did he come from?

Strange people were starting to pop up all over neighborhoods these days. Nationalities that he thought he would never see.

Let alone somebody from India or Pakistan.

He got used to it when he was in the Navy and stationed in New Jersey. That was his first introduction there but here. Indiana? How did they even find it or even know it exists?

Herbert was baffled.

What's the neighbor doing now?

Herbert was enjoying his afternoon nap when he was woken by the sound of lawn mowers.

He looked out the window and saw a lawn company was cutting his neighbor's grass. The neighbor was in his slippers and wearing white pajama pants. He stood off to the side and appeared to be instructing the one on the mower.

Herbert saw the guy mowing roll his eyes as he turned the large mower around the opposite way so as if to try to avoid further instruction.

"Who does this guy think he is?"

"What's that, honey?" She was in the kitchen making him a sandwich for lunch.

"Our neighbor. He has a lawn company cutting the grass."

"Maybe he can't cut the grass. Maybe he has a medical problem."

"I don't think that's what it is."

As if feeling eyes watching him the neighbor looked in Herbert's direction.

"Ohhh, sh...." Herbert ducked away.

"Something wrong?"

"I think he just saw me."

She chuckled. "Maybe he's tired of you staring at him."

"I'm not staring."

"Really? What do you call it then? You've been at this guy since he moved in."

"I'm a considerate and concerned neighbor who's just watching after the community."

"Is that what they're calling stalking these days."

"I'm not stalking. Besides, we don't know who this guy is or where he came from. He could be a serial killer for all we know."

"Now, I think you're getting carried away."

"You know what I mean."

"Now, what's the neighbor doing?"

June rolled over and put the covers over her head. "What is it, Herbert? It's two in the morning."

"Couldn't sleep. Kept hearing this banging sound."

"What?"

"Looks like he's burying something." Herbert watched in amazement as the man dug through the hard Indiana soil in the middle of summer as if he were cutting through butter. On the side of where he was digging was a large black rolled up tarp. "He's up to something."

"I'm sure he is. Now go back to sleep."

Herbert didn't like what the man was up to. Everything about him had suspicious written all over him.

He watched as he rolled the object into the hole and watched on for the next hour as he covered it up.

The next morning the police were down the street. There had been a murder. Mrs. Tucker. The police said it was an attempted robbery but from the looks of things Mrs. Tucker didn't go down without a fight. The police said she managed to get three shots off with one of them hitting the crook.

They said it was too bad that she didn't kill him and he got away.

When Herbert heard this, he knew right away who did this.

But why Mrs. Tucker? She was a nice old lady who kept to herself since her husband, Barney passed away in his sleep two years ago.

She's a tough and rough ole coot though.

Herbert looked at the mound of dirt in the neighbor's yard and wondered if he should call.

After talking to Kyle Clemmons, who lived on the other side of him, Kyle told him his dog Peetes died and the neighbor was kind enough to bury it for him.

That destroyed Herbert's assumptions.

Still though he knew something wasn't right about this guy.

Something was off.

He tried talking to the neighbor again when he saw him out in his yard pulling weeds out of his small flower garden but the neighbor wouldn't seem to give him the time or day.

This infuriated Herbert even more.

Why would he talk to Kyle Clemmons and not him?

June told him he was overreacting and needed to leave the guy alone and that he wasn't bothering anybody. She reminded him that we are innocent until proven guilty.

She told Herbert he never should've retired from the railroad. Gave him way too much time.

Herbert wasn't buying it though. Not at all.

"Something is going to come up. You'll see and you'll see I'm right. I don't know what it is just yet but it will." As he sat in his rocking chair on the front porch.

June rolled her eyes and talked him into coming inside for dinner. "Give the guy a break for a little while."

Herbert wasn't going to rest until he figured this out.

It was late and Herbert was out of beer. After all that had been going on the last thing he needed was to be out of beer.

It was raining and hard to see and the fog wasn't helping either as with the way of the Indiana weather when it gets too humid in July.

He saw the neighbor. AKA squatter.

A woman was screaming in her car as the man looked to be punching her and ran off with her purse.

Herbert ran over and saw it was Beth. Her face was bloody and it looked like she had a broken nose.

"What's the neighbor doing now?" June hated to ask

Herbert's nose was pressing against the window as he tried his best to see but the angle was bad.

There were red and blue flashing lights.

"Looks like they're going to arrest him for what he did?" Bout time we get some justice round here."

"You called the police on him?"

"Bet you ass I did. For what he did. He took a gulp of his beer. "Beating up that ole woman and took her purse."

"You know for a fact it was him?"

"Yep. Had to be him "

"So you're not sure?"

"Pretty sure."

June slapped her forehead.

"Wouldn't believe what the neighbors doing now?"

"I don't think I want to know." She slapped her forehead again which was very quickly becoming a habit.

"He's standing in his front yard smoking a cigarette and acting like nothing's happened."

"What was supposed to have happened?"

"Seriously! He killed that old lady and took her purse."

"Oh yeah that "

"I can't believe he's not in jail "

"Maybe he's innocent."

"No. He's not innocent. I know what I saw. I'm not going to let him get away with this."

"Oh honey. Just stop it."

He paced the floor back and forth like a nervous Nellie."

"What are you looking at now, Herbert?" She saw him peeking out the window.

"Watching the neighbor "

"What's he doing now!" She couldn't wait to see what he came up with.

"Nothing. Just sitting in that chair on the porch "

"And that's a crime?"

"It is when your casing out the neighborhood looking to see who he's going to kill next "

She waved her hand as if this were all foolishness. "I'm sure the poor man is just fine."

"I'm sure he's not. He's making ne nervous. He's been sitting there for three days every day."

"Maybe he likes sitting on his front porch and enjoy the day. More people need to do that if you ask me. "

"Not line he's doing."

The neighbor was up to something. He just knew it and he was going to see to it that nobody else in the neighborhood was going to get killed.

"Oh great. This is just great?"

"What's he doing now, Herbert?"

"He's trimming the hedges."

"Good. It's about time somebody started taking care of that property."

"There's more to it than that. He's only doing it so he can see what's going on in the neighborhood. Watch people come and go "

"Didn't that sounds familiar?" She wasn't surprised he didn't hear her.

"He must be stopped."

"Oh, Herbert Just stop it."

He did his pacing the floor thing. "We can't let him get away with this. He might've fooled the police but he's not fooling me."

"Ohh, Herbert."

"Now this is really getting old "Herbert said.

"What's he doing now, Herbert?"

"I just caught him watching me from his window. He looked right at me and smiled. He's up to something. I just know it. I think he's going to try and kill me "

"Herbert, now you're getting carried away."

"I don't think so. You didn't see the way he was watching me."

"I'm sure he has better things to do than to keep his eye on you "

"I wonder how he's going to do it."

"Do what?"

"Killing me, June, Haven't been listening to a thing I said?"

"I hear you just fine "

"He may try a hammer or use a knife. I know he likes to sneak up on his victims. He likes it quiet. Must've been a specialist in the special forces. And had all that special training and such."

"Now, you're just being plain silly "

"I don't think it's a good idea for you to go outside for a while till this guy is gone. It's just not safe."

June rolled her eyes and went back to the kitchen. "I'm sure he's just fine "

"Nope. Afraid not. You didn't see what I saw. I know what a guy like him is capable of. People like him think they're all slick with the way they walk around all sneaky sneak."

"I don't think he's quite like that."

"Something smells good. What's for supper?"

"I made your favorite. Lasagna"

The doorbell rang.

"Wonder who that could be," Herbert said. We hardly ever get visitors "He pulled the curtain back on the small door window. "June. You're not going to believe this." His heart beating fast as beads of sweat lined his forehead. "I told you he's up to no good."

"Who , Herbert?"

"Our neighbor. He's standing there on our porch trying to break in our house. I warned you," he said waving a finger. "I told you this was going to happen. "

June chuckled at her husband. Stop being silly , Herbert. I invited him for dinner."

Herbert jumped away from the door. "You did what? Are you crazy?"

"I told you , Herbert he was a nice man. I talked to him the other day when you went to the store."

"You talked to him?"

"Sure. He asked if something was wrong because he saw you always watching him out the window. I told him that's just ,Herbert and we both laughed. So, I invited him for dinner. Thought it would be a good idea for you to finally meet our new neighbor "

NO HARD FEELINGS

Cam whacked the asshole in the head with the ball peen hammer the second he came out of the store and no one looking.

Nobody was going to miss this guy.

WHACK WHACK WHACK. He went on his head.

The ball peen hit with a thud.

Cracking sound of scull.

The guy deserved it. Every bit of it. Cam did not like it when people talked to the employees that way. Such a harsh tone like they are better than the one working the counter.

It was a good thing Cam was standing behind the asshole otherwise he would have gotten away with it for sure.

Not many people like Cam that are willing to set people straight.

The man was whispering. Cam was hard hearing so he inched his way up closer so he could hear what he was saying. It didn't sound good. Something about let's go in the back and I'll give you an extra tip.

Cam was like, really? He's going to do this right out here in the open like this?

The young girl, which Cam thought it was nice to see young folks working these days said he didn't have a receipt and it couldn't be this store because they do not carry that particular item.

Mr. asshole started getting loud as he was trying to intimidate her with his loud voice.

Say crap like, 'do you know who I am? Do you have any idea?'

Cam was thinking, no of course not and judging from her expression she didn't either.

He demanded to speak to a manager but the manager came over the radio and said he was back in the stock room and to just go ahead and refund him the money.

So there you go.

He hated to have to do it but it was called for. It is that important.

The man was dressed in a business suit and was probably some executive or some shit. You know, one of those types that thinks he's all that and a bag of chips because he holds some fancy job title.

Fancy job titles mean no purpose was the way Cam saw it.

The man didn't know what hit him.

He bobbed and weaved. The dude's eyes rolled to the back of his head.

"No hard feeling," Cam said. He smirked at his own joke.

Some customers needed to be dealt with.

People gathered around and didn't say anything. They knew the bastard deserved it.

Cam rolled the guy over and looked in his eyes. Blood trickled along his right cheek as his head lay in a puddle of blood.

His blood.

Bastard blood, cam chuckled.

The man looked at him like what was he doing. He looked confused.

"Shouldn't talk to the employees that way," Cam said. "Bad for your health."

"Screw you," the man said and spat blood.

"Now now. You're in no position to be talking shit. Consider a life lesson. These are hard working folks you were talking down to. Nobody likes to be talked down to. They just don't."

"You have nothing to do with this."

"I have everything to do with this. It's my duty to make customers like you treat the working folk with respect. Just to make sure you get the picture we're going to take a little ride."

Cam felt something hit his head. Made a loud thunk thunk sound. It took him a moment to realize somebody was hitting him on the head.

His vision blurred as his knees suddenly felt week before he collapsed.

He saw who was hitting him. It was that young girl he rescued from that idiot. A hammer hit him in the face. His teeth. He wasn't sure but he was certain she knocked his two front teeth out.

"Why are you doing this?" He tried to say but his speech came out slurred and spitting blood.

She whacked him again and again.

"No hard feelings," she said. "But that was my father."

HANGRY PAINS

Welcome to Red and Rare Fatty's Cuts. The sign read. Red and Rare Fatty's Cuts was known to be the best steak house in Indiana.

The place had some lovely wood framework on the inside.

There were about thirty tables in the main dining room and he could see a wing branched off to the left which opened into another dining area only a little smaller.

On the left just as walked in was a clear case full of various cuts of meat.

Porterhouse. Ribeye, sirloin and a lot of filet mignon.

Behind the case a young woman was mixing dough in a giant stainless steel tub.

He followed the hostess to his table.

He passed a giant steer head on the left side and various pictures of cowboys and some of the celebrities who had visited in the past.

Since he was in town for a business meeting, he thought he would stop by and see what all the fuss was about.

He had ordered the special cut Fatty's Top Sirloin cooked well done.

His mouth watered for it.

His gut ached for it.

When she placed it in front of him. Well.

He did not like the looks of it.

He poked it with his fork. "This steak does t look cooked "

The waitress was a young hot chick with big boobs. Black eye shadow around her eyes. She had on long leather boots. Heather was on her name tag. She looked like a Heather. "It's what you ordered, sir."

"It's not what I ordered. I ordered my steak medium rare. He poked it with a fork and held it up. "This is raw."

"I'm sorry, sir. I'll take it back to the cook and he'll make you another one. So sorry for this."

Colton, not happy with the way things have been handled so far but at least they were willing to make it up. Probably get a free meal out of it now.

It was too bad, Veronica wasn't here. His wife. He missed her terribly. Damn cancer. He had never been the same since. Also, when they went to restaurants they never got the order wrong when she was with him.

Weird.

Mistakes happen. Looking around the place had about a hundred people. Waitresses running back and forth fetching drinks and carrying dishes and hot plates. It was a busy night.

He drank the rest of his iced tea. The salty peanuts made him drink more. All around him people drank beer and other fancy drinks.

Stupid restaurants. They feed you salty food on purpose so you drink more. He heard from a friend of his that was in the restaurant business.

He would have to give her a bigger tip for being rude. He didn't mean to be. He hoped she wouldn't take it hard. He thought he would explain when she returned.

The waitress was walking toward his table. Carrying a plate. Looked like a cooked steak.

Maybe that was mine, he thought.

She placed it in front of the fat guy sitting at the table in front of him.

Great. Stomach rumbled. Feeling hangry pains. Not fun.

"Heather."

She looked. Smiled. She had a pretty smile he'd give her that. Pretty too. He liked the goth look. "Be there in a second, sir."

He watched her butt as she walked back quickly toward the kitchen. Probably fetching his steak.

He needed to get her attention.

That's okay. She'll be back for another round soon. He hoped she wasn't ignoring him because she didn't think he was going to tip well. Veronica was good at tipping. She always knew exactly what to give and how much. He was never good at math. Even simple math made his head hurt.

Something banged on his seat and hit him in the head.

He turned.

Some young kid, five-year-old at the most was playing around in his seat. "Sorry about that, Sir," the mother said.

She was pretty too. Long black hair. Thin. He noticed her husband was fat too. Amazing how many young skinny women like fat dudes. Opposite for him. His wife was fat.

Hmm. Funny how things work that way.

Not funny how he hadn't gotten his steak yet. What are they killing the cow?

He glanced around. It seemed that everybody else had gotten their steaks or chicken. It's either steak or chicken in most of these place now-a-days. He even got here before the fat man in front and he'd already gotten his steak. Heck he was almost finished.

Should've brought a woman with me. More people means more of a tip.

Instead of just sitting there looking like an idiot staring out in space watching everybody eating their steaks he pulled his phone out of his pocket and decided to check his e-mail.

Waste of time. Some of these places sure know how to waste your time.

All junk mail and stupid articles.

Lately, most of it has been about that sub implosion. Too bad for them the CEO was an idiot. He felt sorry for the nineteen-year-old who didn't seem to have much of a choice in the whole thing.

Another article about how to get what you want in life in five easy steps.

Hmmm. Comical. Nobody gets what they want in life these days. Life just plain sucks.

That's what the problem with the world is these days. Everybody thinks they have to be happy all the time and if they're not then somebody always has to show up and tell them they're wrong for feeling that way.

Screw you. That's what he has to say to those folks.

Now, I want my steak.

He thought about getting up and leaving. Go some place else. With his luck he'll pass the waitress on the way out on her way to deliver his steak.

More stomach rumbling.

He thought he would finally dip into a slice of bread with butter even though he was trying to watch his carbs. Every time he tries to do something special for himself like eating healthy or exercising something always has to come up and wreck his plans. Some times you just can't win.

Tonight is not going to be that night. Tonight he is going to get his steak. Tonight he will win even if he has to say here all night.

A young couple sitting in the booth beside him. Young dude looked like he was in college. Sitting across from him was a pretty red head. They were holding hands and talking about how they were going to have a nice house with kids and how their life is going to be so great.

Hmmm. He wanted to clue the hopeless romantic in that marriage life doesn't work that way. Sure, it may for the first couple years. Until life sets in bombarding them with all its problems.

He wondered how her family was because he wanted to tell him that you are not just marrying her but you are marrying the entire family. Love'm or hate'm. They're yours.

Things go okay for a while then the mother-in-law dies.

Oh well. Not really a bad thing. If she was anything like his mother-in-law it wasn't a bad thing. May she rest in peace.

Next comes the kid that disrupts their life and all of a sudden the sex becomes bare minimum and soon he will be having an affair, probably with her best friend.

He leaned over and kissed her.

How sweet. Romantic.

The waitress placed their steaks in front of them. Nice sized steaks. Perfectly cooked.

Okay, he thought. Where's mine. I was here before they were.

Did they forget? Did my order get lost in the system.

Oh, yes. The system. He didn't want to even get started on the system.

He heard the waitress tell them to enjoy their meals and let her know if they need anything.

They nodded and said everything looked fine.

Not fine for him.

He hadn't gotten his steak yet.

"Excuse me. Heather?" Making sure he was nice even though his insides were boiling. Get more with sugar.

"Yes?"

"How's my meal coming?"

"The cook is working on it. It should be out shortly." She had a lovely smile. Pretty.

"It's just that's it been a while. Thought may my order got lost in the system considering how busy you are."

He noticed a look of frustration on the waitress's face. "Yes. Well. We're a little backed up right now. Besides. You're order was done but you sent it back."

"That's because it wasn't done."

"Well, the cook looked at it and said it was fine."

"It was raw."

"Sir, we don't deliver raw meat here. All of our steaks our cooked to suit your taste. Now, it may have been a little under cooked but not raw."

"It was bleeding." He couldn't believe she was arguing with him about this. The steak was so raw it was mooing.

"We'll get back to you shortly, sir. In the meantime can I get you another drink." She glanced at his empty glass. "Iced tea wasn't it?"

"Yes. Please."

He watched her butt wiggle and jiggle as she walked off. He realizes he's no spring chicken but kids these days have no concept of what customer service is all about.

Oddly enough, she returned quickly with his iced tea. "I'll check with our cook to see how it's coming."

"Thank you."

"It's my pleasure."

He cringed. He wishes people would stop saying that.

He sipped his tea. Tasted bitter. No sugar. No lemon. He spat it out. Now he was getting really frustrated. Everything that could go wrong was going wrong.

Heather will be passing by soon. Probably not to check on him but to check on the romantic loving couple beside him. They seemed to be enjoying their steaks and having some nice conversation.

Lovely.

The place was getting busier and busier. Well, such is the way on a Friday night. Everybody out to enjoy and nice meal.

Except him.

Cause he hadn't gotten his steak yet.

Thinking about leaving again.

He watched the fat guy sitting at two tables in front of the romantic couple chewing his steak. Nice and slow. Savoring each tiny chew. Colton watched the way the man cut each slither precisely and couldn't help but notice how each slice was the same perfect size.

What do they call that? OCD or something like that.

The man placed the piece in his mouth. A little trickle of juice ran down the corner of his lip as he talked to what was probably his wife. Everything about the man was nearly to perfect measure except for the way he was talking with his mouth full showing his seafood. Colton had to look away.

The cacophony of clinking of forks on plates, spoons in bowls and knives slicing across the dishes was irritating.

Heather smiled at him as she passed by on her way to another table.

He raised his hand.

"Yes, Sir." Irritated tone in her voice.

"My tea is unsweetened. I asked for sweetened."

"Ohh, I'm sorry. I thought you said you wanted it unsweetened."

He wanted to say how more clear did he have to be. It seemed that this place was getting everything all wrong. Completely wrong.

He also asked about his steak.

"I'll check on that right away, sir. I'm sure the cook is done with it by now. Should have it out to you shortly."

He wanted to say he sure hoped so. He had to be careful not to be rude. Restaurant folks can do all sorts of things to your food if you piss them off.

Like spit in it.

Throw it on the floor and place it back on the griddle.

Wipe it on their ass.

Some may even piss on it.

He chuckled. It reminded him of the time he was in the Navy and the Officer of the Deck, who he didn't like and gave everyone a hard time ordered him to fetch him a cup of coffee.

He fetched him a cup of joe all right. Did the little trick sailors call dirty dicking where they rub the coffee cup with their penis followed up with a splash of pubic hairs that nobody will ever notice.

So yes. Be nice to your servers.

Though after this visit he didn't think he was going to be coming back.

Maybe should go back to drinking. Naa. Drinking makes things worse.

Just want my steak.

Seriously, this wasn't making any sense.

More and more people were coming and going. He watched them get their food, eat and leave.

Yet. Still here.

Haven't gotten his steak yet.

"Just checking on my steak." He asked Heather.

"Coming right up, Sir."

"Thank you so much." So hungry he could eat the entire cow.

Five minutes later he saw Heather walking down the aisle toward his table carrying a delicious steak on a plate.

It was smoking.

He could smell the spices.

Ahhh, Yes. Fresh off the grill.

The way she smiled as she walked toward told him he knew it was his. All his.

Just bring that puppy right over here.

He was so hungry he could've eaten the fat man at the table in front of him. All six hundred pounds worth.

His hangry pains coming to an end.

His mouth watered. Stomach growled.

The steak nice and juicy as he savored the aroma of the various spices.

She sat the steak in of him. "The moment has finally arrived."

He looked at. Bit his lower lip. Poked it with a fork."

"Something wrong, sir?"

Charred on the outside but when he cut a sliver it was very very pink.

"It's only half cooked.'

"Sir. It's just how you wanted it."

He cut off another sliver of steak and held it up. "Does this look cooked to you?"

"Sir, this is how our chef cooks his steaks. As you are aware, I'm sure, Red and Rare Fatty's Cuts is a very popular steak house here. Our chef only uses the finest cuts of beef, grown and raised on his very own family's cattle farm. Each steak is cut precisely a half inch thick which allows for a more thorough cooking. Our chef has won numerous awards and is the most sought after chef in all the Midwest. Our chef seasons his steaks with over twenty various secret spices all imported from all over the world. He uses the finest of grills to be sure nothing is over or undercooked."

He was trying his best to keep his voice down to try not make a scene. The waitress was talking loud.

Everybody stopped chewing on their steaks. The cacophony of knives and forks hitting plates ceased as the entire place fell silent as they all looked at him as if he had just committed the worst sin ever.

Heather smiled. "Well, sir. We certainly do not want you to be unhappy, so I'll just take it back to the chef and he'll fix you right up."

"Whhoaaaaaa." Everyone in the restaurant said in unison.

All of a sudden, he did not get a good feeling about this.

What was going on? Surely, he couldn't be the only one that was unhappy with the way the chef cooked their steaks.

"Are you sure the chef cooked it and not a beginner?" Colton asked.

Once again, the restaurant went, whhoaaaaaa.

"Ahem." She cleared her throat. "That wasn't a very nice thing to say, sir."

"I didn't realize I said anything that bad."

"You called Chef Hackasaki a beginner."

"I didn't not call him a beginner. I simply asked if you were sure it wasn't done by a new employee or a trainee perhaps."

"Word famous chef Hackasaki doesn't use trainees to cook his award winning meals."

Colton put his hand up. "You'll have to excuse me. I didn't mean to insult the chef my any means. I Just thought maybe he had somebody new working back there with him is all."

"Chef Hackasaki is the only one in his kitchen."

First he was having a hard time believing that the chef was cooking all these meals by himself. No way was he going to challenge the waitress and add any more flavor to the insults.

"I'll take this back to the chef. He's not going to like having his specially grilled with various imported spices made to award winning perfection."

"I'm sorry. But I just like it a little more done."

"And the chef will take care of that. He may come out to talk to you."

"That wouldn't be necessary."

"Chef Hackasaki takes his cooking very serious." Her tone sounded demonic.

He hoped the chef wasn't insulted by any of this by no means. He never meant to insult anyone especially a world famous chef, though he wasn't sure how this chef got the title of world famous. He never heard of this chef Hackasaki. Seriously, how can anyone forget a name like that.

People stopped staring at him and went back to chewing on their special award winning steaks. Some seemed looked to be savoring each moment.

Seemed he was the only one that didn't get his.

A loud bang in the back coming from the kitchen.

Dishes breaking. Crashing.

Someone yelling in a foreign language that sounded Chinese.

He wondered if it was the chef and he was pissed at the waitress. Lord, he hoped he wasn't taking it out on her. She didn't deserve any of this.

He thought maybe he should go in the back and ask to speak with the chef to clear things all up.

Maybe it was a good thing if he did come out and speak with him about his award winning steaks.

There seemed to be a lot of commotion coming from the bar as people stepped aside and cleared a path.

He saw the chef's white hat above the crowd.

Chairs tipping over.

People screaming. Running. Arms flailing as they appeared to be running from a mass shooter or someone yelled the famous word bomb.

A meat clever slammed on top of a pretty blonde woman's head splitting it in two. Her eyes wide with shock.

Standing at the edge of the bar with meat cleaver in hand was the world famous chef, Chef Hackasaki.

Foaming at the mouth. Face red.

Slicing aimlessly at whoever was in his path.

He sliced off a woman's head who unfortunately was not able to get out of the way.

Poor woman.

The chef screeching, screaming in a Chinese yell as if Colton was watching one of those old Japanese films with dubbed English.

Chef Hackasaki looked at Colton as if he already knew who he was.

"Chef Hackasaki doesn't like you returning his finely grilled steaks with various imported seasonings all done to perfection."

Colton put his hands up in surrender. "Sir, I ..."

Colton wanted to apologize but the chef cut him off. "Silence."

The chef held two meat cleavers as he waved them back and forth performing various tricks as if they were numb chucks.

Colton saw several people watching this outside through the window.

Some hidden behind tables.

They changed for the chef. Urging him on and on. It was as if they were enjoying this as if it were a show for their entertainment.

Chef Hackasaki said "Choo Choo train." He made locomotive sounds as he performed some trick with smoke coming out of his ears as he chugged in circles around Colton as he performed his amazing feats.

His cleaver swiped across the face of some sixty something old man who wasn't fast enough or the reflexes to dodge Chef Hackasaki's amazing skills.

The crowd cheered as blood splattered over the chef's white apron.

The crowd cheered for more.

"Chop Suey!" Chef yelled. He now spoke in English but his mouth moved much faster.

This was weird like watching a poorly dubbed foreign film.

He pointed his cleaver at Colton. Colton grabbed a knife off a table and threw it at the chef.

The chef dodged it with the ease of a ninja.

Another knife. Spoon. Silly yes, but at this stage he had to throw what he could get.

The chef pinged them off with his cleaver.

Spoon. Knife. Coffee cup

Ping...Ping...Ping...

World famous chef Hackasaki, this was child's play.

Colton really didn't expect to hit the chef, though it would be nice if he could manage to slow him down. He had feeling he wasn't going to make it out of here alive.

People continued to watch as if it were all for show.

Colton could hear everyone chanting for chef Hackasaki.

Recording all the festivities on their phones.

Why not? Whoever posts this on YouTube is guaranteed around several thousand hits.

Nothing is safe and private these days.

Would be nice if several good Samaritans would step in. No way could the chef take them all.

People continued to chant for the chef.

He managed to back up to the door.

Exhaled a sigh of relief. Pushed it.

Locked.

He tried the other door.

Locked.

A crowd of people stood in the entry way. All of them chanting for the chef.

This was surreal.

Could this really be happening?

They weren't letting him leave.

Chef Hackasaki twirled his cleavers as he said something in Chinese in which Colton had no idea what he was saying. His lips moving faster than the words that came out.

The chef grunted a few HiiiiiYaaaas as he chucked a cleaver. Colton managed to grab one of the smaller square tables and blocked it.

The cleaver stuck in the table just inches from his head.

The chef produced another cleaver from under his blood splattered apron. It was like he had a never-ending supply.

Colton looked around trying to figure a way out of here.

The kitchen.

Great

Crank the gas up on the hibachi grills. He cranked the knob on high.

He saw lighter fluid by the base of the grill.

Now we're talking.

At least he thought it was lighter fluid. Probably not that but he'd seen the chefs use it to light a flame.

It was a small white plastic old ketchup bottle.

The chef chucked a cleaver at him, this time he wasn't able to get out of the way and it sliced him across the left forearm. Colton backed against the wall.

Chef Hackasaki grinned evil like as if he was finally able to capture his prize.

Colton was lime a mouse cornered by a boa constrictor.

The chef approved and Colton drenched him with the fluid.

The chef yelling. Arms waving.

Colton grabbed his lighter from his left pocket and gave the Bic an ole flick tossed it at the Chef. In seconds the chef was in flames.

Yelling something incoherent in Chinese. Chefs' arms flailing and tumbled over the dining table.

This gave him enough time to get out running past the crowd leaving a screaming chef behind.

Two days later he saw on the news.

World famous chef Hackasaki had died. Killed by a fire.

Colton thought for sure something more was going to come of it especially with the amount of people recording it.

It never did. Either that or it was going to take a while for things to catch up.

A year later, Colton finally started getting out of the house again. He thought he would go out and get back in the world.

He stops at a steakhouse.

It was new in town.

"Just opened three days ago," a man said. He was with what appeared to be his wife and five-year-old son. "Said some award-winning steak chef just opened it up."

That caught Colton's attention. "Award winning you say?"

"Supposed to be the best in the nation."

"No thanks. I'll have to pass on this one. Steak really isn't my thing."

Don't miss out!

Visit the website below and you can sign up to receive emails whenever Christopher Ridge publishes a new book. There's no charge and no obligation.

https://books2read.com/r/B-A-RYTC-HCSLC

BOOKS 2 READ

Connecting independent readers to independent writers.

Did you love *Shredded Bodies*? Then you should read *Shouldn't Play with Dead Things*[1] by Christopher Ridge!

[2]

A five story collection of short dark humorous horror stories. If you like dark humor and gory, these tales may be for you.
Read more at creaturecritter.blogspot.com.

---

1. https://books2read.com/u/49ddYY

2. https://books2read.com/u/49ddYY

Also by Christopher Ridge

Hairy Scary Eight Legged Engineers
HOME INVASION
Bug Spray not Included
DateBite
Giant Steel Death Machines
The Ugly Truth About Shopping Carts
Dead End Job
Lobster Woman of Bubwater
Hatchet Hall
There's a Man on that Street
CUT'M UP TALES
Severance
The Fling
Macabrre Monthly
Strikeout
Splat
Slime
Because Google Said
Demented Tales
Captive
The Ghost Pirate
Clickety Clackers
Bumper to Bumper

The Hatch
Help Wanted
Creatures
Shouldn't Play with Dead Things
Sickies
Shredded Bodies

Watch for more at creaturecritter.blogspot.com.

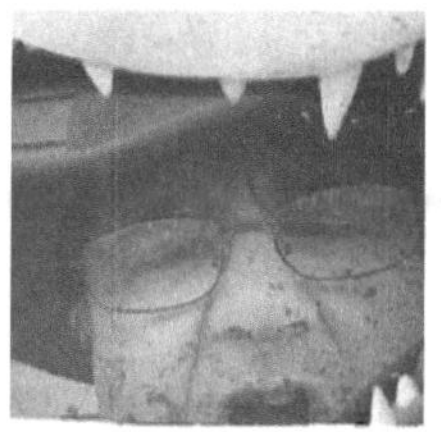

About the Author

Christopher Ridge is a creature feature horror and sci-fi writer. He enjoys B horror movies, aliens, monsters and mutant insects and such. To get an idea of what his stories and short novels are like think ATTACK OF THE KILLER TOMATOES, THEM, and IT CAME FROM OUTER SPACE. He lives in Indianapolis Indiana with his wife and two sons.

Read more at creaturecritter.blogspot.com.